Also by Jean Ure:

ORCHARD SUPER CRUNCHIES:

SANDY SIMMONS

Sandy Simmons Superstar!
Sandy Simmons – Sweet Success
Sandy Simmons Saves the Day!
Sandy Simmons and the Spotlight Spook
Sandy Simmons – Show Stealer

WOODSIDE SCHOOL
The Fright
King of Spuds
Loud Mouth
Soppy Birthday
Who's for the Zoo?
Who's Talking?

ORCHARD BLACK APPLES:

Just Sixteen
Love is Forever

e

c

Sandy Simmons

☆ STAR STRUCK! ☆

Jean Ure

Illustrated by Peter Kavanagh

ORCHARD BOOKS

For Ena,
with even more love
P.K.

ORCHARD BOOKS
96 Leonard Street, London EC2A 4XD
Orchard Books Australia
14 Mars Road, Lane Cove, NSW 2066
First published in Great Britain in 2000
First paperback edition 2000
Text © Jean Ure, 2000
Illustrations © Peter Kavanagh, 2000
The rights of Jean Ure to be identified as the author
and Peter Kavanagh as the illustrator of this work
have been asserted by them in accordance with the
Copyright, Designs and Patents Act, 1988.
A CIP catalogue record for this book is available
from the British Library.
1 86039 570 8 (hbk)
1 84121 025 0 (pbk)
1 3 5 7 9 10 8 6 4 2 (hbk)
1 3 5 7 9 10 8 6 4 2 (pbk)
Printed in Great Britain

CONTENTS

Chapter one   9

Chapter two   21

Chapter three   36

Chapter four   47

Chapter five   59

Chapter six   70

Chapter one

Sandy Simmons SUPERSTAR

I write this everywhere! All over the place.
In my school books, in my diary, in the
snow. Even on my bedroom wall! I am not
just going to be a ★S★T★A★R★ I am going
to be a ★SUPERSTAR★

It is my big ambition in life.

So you can imagine how I felt when one
day my mum told me that I was going to
have to leave stage school. I couldn't
believe it! Leave Starlight? It had to be
some kind of bad dream!

But it wasn't a dream; it was horrid reality. Mum explained to me how Dad's business had been doing really badly and he was going to have to close it down and find some other kind of job. If he could. Mum didn't seem too hopeful.

"You see, Sandy, your dad's not a young man any more. He's over forty. There aren't that many jobs for older people."

I could see that being over forty made you pretty ancient. But Mum wasn't over forty!

"You're still young," I told her. "You could get a job!"

Mum said that she was certainly going to look for one.

"But even if we both manage to find something, I'm afraid there still won't be enough money to pay your fees at Starlight. It costs a lot to send you to a stage school."

"You could use the money I earned from the Frooties ad!" I said.

I'd done this commercial a little while ago and Mum and Dad had made me put all the money in the building society for when I was older. But why wait till I was older? I needed it now, so I could stay on at Starlight!

But Mum shook her head and said that what I'd earned from the Frooties ad would only be enough for just one term.

"So I could stay on for next term, at least," I said. "And then maybe I'd get another ad, and then another one, and—"

"I'm sorry, Sandy. It would just put too much pressure on you," said Mum. "And in the long run it would only make things worse. Better you leave now, at the end of the school year. It won't be so bad! You can go to The Chase and meet up again with all your old friends from primary school."

I didn't want to go to The Chase! The Chase is an ordinary *boring* school. They don't do Mime, or Voice, or Movement. They don't send you for auditions. How could I be a superstar if I went to The Chase?

Mum said soothingly that maybe when I finished school I would be able to go somewhere like the Royal Academy of Dramatic Art and study. And in the meantime, perhaps, Dad would let me use my building-society money to pay for acting classes on a Saturday morning.

"That's no good!" I roared.

It would be years and *years* before I finished school. By that time all my friends from Starlight – Dell and Sash and Rosa – would be real professionals, working in the business. They would be in musicals, they would be on telly, they would be going off on tour. Oh, I couldn't bear it!

Mum said again about having classes on a Saturday morning. But it wouldn't be the same! Classes on a Saturday were for amateurs. People who were just doing it for fun. I was serious!

"Sandy, sweetie, I'm sorry," said Mum. "I know how much it means to you."

"You don't!" I sobbed. "You can't possibly!"

"Darling, I do! Your dad and I both feel terrible about it. Unfortunately, it's just one of those things."

"It's not fair!"

"Life isn't always fair," said Mum. "Think of all those children who can't even go to Saturday-morning classes!"

I didn't care about them. I only cared about me!

Mum sighed and said that it was going to be hard for all of us.

"Especially your dad. So please, Sandy! Try to be brave. I don't want you making your dad feel worse than he already does."

I felt like screaming, 'Never mind Dad! What about me?'

"My entire life is going to be ruined," I told Mum.

14

And I ran upstairs to my bedroom and slammed the door behind me. "I might as well be dead!" I threw myself on to my bed and buried my head in the pillow. How could I go back to an ordinary school after being at Starlight? Starlight made me feel so special! I loved the red cloaks that we wore in winter. I loved walking down the road with Sash to catch the tube every morning. I loved everyone knowing that we were stage-school students. I just loved everything about it! The tap shoes, the ballet shoes, the leotards, the greasepaint – everything!

I suddenly remembered Rosa, last term.

Her mum had told her that *she* was going to have to leave. I'd felt so sorry for her! I'd never dreamt that the very same thing would soon be happening to me…

Tears went squelching into my pillow. Rosa's mum had been mad at her because she'd left a tap running in the bathroom and practically flooded the house. That was why Rosa was going to have to leave. But I hadn't left any taps running! I hadn't done anything! It was all so unfair!

Rosa's mum had forgiven her, in the end. She'd discovered she was having a baby – *two* babies, in fact! She was having *twins* – and it had made her so happy she'd told Rosa she could stay.

I couldn't see my mum suddenly discovering she was having twins and being happy about it. Not if Dad was going to be out of work and we didn't have any money.

My life was falling to pieces and there was nothing I could do about it!

I heard footsteps thudding up the stairs. My brother, Thomas. He always thuds and bangs.

Next thing I knew, he was hammering on my door.

"Hey! Sandy!"

"Go away!" I snarled.

"But I want to talk to you!"

"Well, I don't want to talk to you! Just go away!" I flipped over on to my back and smothered my face with the pillow. "Gowaylivlone!"

"You what?" said Thomas.

I screamed, and sprang into a sitting position. I shouted, "Go boil yourself, frog face!" and hurled my pillow at the door.

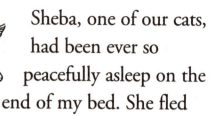 Sheba, one of our cats, had been ever so peacefully asleep on the end of my bed. She fled with a yowl of fright as the pillow went flumping past her.

That made me feel mean. My life might have been shattered beyond all hope of repair, but I didn't have to take it out on a poor little innocent cat.

"You still there?" said Thomas, from the other side of the door.

I felt like screaming, "Where do you think I am? In outer space?" But I was suddenly remembering Rosa again. We'd all been dead worried about her. We couldn't understand why she was being so ratty with everyone. Now I was being ratty with Thomas. And frightening poor Sheba! So

I didn't scream. Instead, I found a hankie and blodged at my eyes and muttered. "You can come in if you want."

Thomas pushed the door open just the tiniest crack and sort of slinked his way through. He has no idea how to make an entrance! He'll never be an actor. But that's all right 'cos he doesn't want to be. Thomas is the brains of the family, I am the creative one.

Thomas mumbled, "Mum just told me."

I didn't say anything: I couldn't. I knew if I tried I'd start crying all over again, and I just hate crying in front of people.

"I'm sorry," said Thomas gruffly. "I wish there was something I could do."

"Well, there isn't." I didn't mean to say it ungraciously. It just came out that way.

Thomas frowned. He scooped up Sheba, who was mewing piteously round his legs. Telling him how horrid I'd been to her!

"I know it sounds like your life has come to an end," he said, "but you'll still be a star!"

I sniffed, dolefully.

"Do you really think so?"

"I'm telling you!" said Thomas. "You know what Auntie Lily says…'if you've got what it takes, you'll get there!'"

Chapter two

There are times when I feel like bashing
and hashing at Thomas. Times when I
could cheerfully *mash him to a pulp*.

There are other times when I think he is
the very best brother in the whole world.

It really made me glow, him
saying that I'd still be a star!
I went away and wrote
Sandy Simmons Superstar
over everything I could find
– including the chalk board
that Mum keeps in the
kitchen for making
shopping lists on.

"That's the spirit!" said Mum. "After all, think of all those big names who've never been to a drama school in their life!"

"Which ones?" I said. But of course Mum couldn't think of a single solitary person, could she?

Dad, trying to cheer me up, said that nobody could teach you how to act.

"You've either got it or you haven't."

"And we all agree that you *have*," said Mum.

I went to bed feeling a bit better and determined that I would make it to the top *no matter what*. I would do what Mum said and go to Saturday morning classes, and I would be the ⋆S⋆T⋆A⋆R⋆ because of having been to stage school and being serious about it, and one day (when I'd been there about six months) they would put on a show and a top movie director would come and see it and – Hey presto! Bingo! Wham! That would be IT. I'd be whizzed off to Hollywood  and given a whopping big contract worth millions of dollars. We would all be rich as could be and Dad would never have to worry about working ever again.

Unfortunately, when I woke up in the morning it all seemed like a silly childish daydream. No one was going to whizz me off to Hollywood. I would be left to moulder at a boring ordinary school doing boring ordinary lessons and every time I looked at the television and saw someone my own age I would feel like howling.

I would just be so *jealous*. I would be *green*.

Especially if it was Starlotta.

Starlotta was a girl in my class at Starlight. She thought she was the cat's whiskers. The fairy on the Christmas tree. The icing on the cake. All because she had an uncle that was in a TV soap. I couldn't bear for Starlotta to know that my dad had lost all his money and I was going to have to leave!

I met Sash as usual and we walked to the tube station. Sash couldn't understand why I was so glum.

"Do cheer up!" she said. "You look as if you've just been up for the lead part and been given the understudy!"

I tried not to snap at her, because after all it wasn't her fault. I heaved a sigh and said, "I've got something to tell you."

"What?"

"Not now," I said. "Later."

Rosa had hugged her terrible secret to herself. It wasn't till I'd found her crying in the cloakroom one day that I'd discovered what was wrong. I'd told her that talking about it would help. Now it was me that had a terrible secret – and I wasn't sure that talking *would* help. But Sash is my best friend. I couldn't keep it from her.

It was raining at first break and we were allowed to stay in school. We were *supposed* to stay in the hall or in our classrooms, but I whispered to Sash to come down to the cloakroom.

"What about the others?" she said.

I hesitated, then I said, "Yes, all right. Them too."

We were all friends – me and Sash, Dell and Rosa. Friends are meant to share. Bad things as well as good.

We scuttled down to the cloakroom making sure that no one saw us. We are not really allowed to sit about down there. I don't know why; in case there's a fire or something, maybe. They like to know where people are. Anyway, it's where we always go if we want to be secret.

Rosa perched on one of the wash-basins, Dell and Sash sat on a hot-water pipe. I scrunched myself up on the window-sill, hugging my knees to my chin just like Rosa had, the day I found her crying.

"Sand's got something to tell us," said Sash.

Rosa took one look at my face and howled, "Oh, no! Your parents are emigrating!"

She said this because one of her cousins had just gone to Australia. Now she expected everybody to be going there!

"Why always think the worst?" said Dell. "It could be something nice!"

"Yes, like she's suddenly been offered this fabulous part on telly," said Sash.

She looked at me, hopefully, but slowly I shook my head. They all sat there, waiting for me to say something. I gulped, took a

deep, deep breath and let it all come
rushing out.

"My dad's shut down his business
'cos it's not making any money
and it means I've got to leave!"

There was a shocked silence.

"Oh, *Sand!*" cried Sasha.

"You can't!" wailed Rosa.

"This is really serious," said Dell.

"I know." I hiccuped, miserably. "It's the
worst thing that's ever happened to me."

"Maybe," said Sasha, "they'll change their
minds?"

"Like mine did," said Rosa.

"Maybe your dad could start
a different sort of business,"
suggested Dell.

"Yes, or go and work for
someone else," said Sash.

"I don't think so," I said. "He's too old…
he's over forty."

A curtain of black gloom descended
upon us.

"Maybe" – Rosa brightened – "maybe
he could come and help my dad in his
sandwich bar!"

"He doesn't know anything about
sandwiches," I said. "He can't even boil an
egg. That's what my mum says."

"There's got to be something," said Sash.
"You can't leave Starlight!"

I blinked and tilted my
chin a bit higher so the
tears couldn't drip off it.

"My dad's already written
a letter…he's told Miss
Todd they're taking me
away at the end of this term."

"This is just *awful*!" yelped Sash.

"I can't bear it!" said Rosa.

"We're the Gang of Four," said Dell.

It is a great comfort to have friends who care about you, but there wasn't anything, alas, that they could actually do. It wasn't like when we'd raised money to help the poor cats of Cats' Cottage when they ran out of funds. We couldn't *ever* raise enough money to pay for my school fees.

The bell rang for the end of break and we all dismally peeled ourselves away from the hot-water pipes and the wash-basin and the window-sill and trailed back out into the corridor. We had walked as far as the stairs that led up to our classroom when I heard a door bang. I turned, and saw Starlotta coming out of the cloakroom. She had been there all the time! Hiding behind a

row of pegs, or shut away behind a door.
She must have heard everything we had
been saying!

"How low can you sink?" said Sasha.

Rosa sniffed. "Only what
you'd expect of her."

Rosa couldn't stand
Starlotta. None of
us really liked her. I
absolutely *hated* the thought
of her knowing about me
having to leave Starlight.

"I bet she goes and tells everyone," I said.
"I bet she gloats!"

But she didn't. She didn't say a word!
I was really amazed. I mean, gloating is
what she loves best. Of course she would
have to admit she'd been eavesdropping,
but she'd have found a way to do it.

"I'm so-o-o sorry, Sandy! I couldn't help overhearing. How simply terrible for you! I would just die if I had to leave Starlight."

That's the sort of thing I would have expected. Instead, she just gave me this strange little pale smile. Well, her face was pale. The smile was little. And strange. What was she smiling at me for? It was like she was saying, "Don't worry! Your secret is safe with me."

Really weird.

And then, the next day, all was revealed. I discovered why she hadn't gloated.

First thing after lunch I was called to see Miss Todd. I'm usually a bit apprehensive when I go and see Miss Todd as I am always wondering to myself what I have done wrong. This time I knew that I hadn't done anything wrong. She was calling me in because of Dad's letter.

"Sandy," she said. "Take a seat! I was sorry to hear that you might have to be leaving us."

Might have to be? My ears pricked up!

"I wonder," said Miss Todd, "if you've considered trying for a scholarship?"

Well! It was the first I'd ever heard of a scholarship.

"The British Drama Foundation awards one scholarship a year to every school that's a member. I'd be very happy to put you in for it, if you think your parents would agree."

"They would!" I said.

They had to! It was my only chance.

"I'll discuss the details with them," said Miss Todd. "There's only one other candidate from the school, and that's Starlotta."

Starlotta??? I think my jaw must have dropped open, or maybe I looked like a person that's had a ton of bricks dropped on their head. "I know only one of you can be successful," said Miss Todd, "but I do think it's worth a go. After all" – she smiled at me – "what have you to lose?"

"N-nothing," I stammered.

"Exactly!" said Miss Todd. "Nothing to lose, and everything to gain. Off you go! I'll have a word with your parents."

I left Miss Todd's office and went racing back down the corridor. I couldn't wait to tell the others! I was going to try for a scholarship!

Yes, and so was Starlotta...

Chapter three

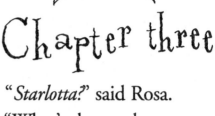

"*Starlotta?*" said Rosa. "What's she need a scholarship for?"

I'd told them about it as I didn't think it was a secret. I mean, Miss Todd hadn't said not to tell people. And everyone was going to know about me! Now that I was trying for a scholarship, I didn't mind who got to hear of it.

"*Her* dad isn't out of work," said Rosa, "is he?"

"She hasn't got a dad," said Sash. "Her mum's divorced."

There was a bit of a silence at this. None of us had realised Starlotta hadn't got a dad. Then Rosa muttered. "Not surprised her mum's divorced if she's anything like Starlotta. Who'd want to live with it?"

"And anyway," said Dell, "what about her uncle?"

Starlotta's famous uncle that was on the telly. Why couldn't he pay for her?

"He must be rich as rich," I said.

"Rolling in it," said Rosa.

"I'm sure if Auntie Lily was rich, she'd pay for me," I said.

Unfortunately, my Auntie Lily doesn't have any money. She always says she never had the knack of making it. Whenever she gets any, like if a little checky-poo arrives

(checky-poo is what she calls a cheque) she immediately puts it in her knickers for fear of losing it. She is a little bit peculiar, but she is my very favourite auntie.

"Are you sure she wouldn't pay?" said Sasha, later, as we travelled home on the tube.

"She couldn't afford to," I said. "She is permanently brassic."

Brassic is what Auntie Lily says when she means broke. When she doesn't have *a bean*.

Sasha sighed. "It is such a nuisance! Why does Starlotta's uncle have to be so stingy?"

I knew what she was trying to say. She was trying to say that if only Starlotta's uncle would pay for her, Starlotta wouldn't have to compete with me for a scholarship.

And if Starlotta wasn't competing, I would stand a far better chance of getting one.

I mean, it wouldn't be absolutely certain, because I would still have to convince the judges I was worth it; but at least I wouldn't have to convince them that I was more worth it than Starlotta!

"Maybe," I suggested, "her uncle doesn't really like her?"

"Who does?" muttered Sasha. "Maybe he just doesn't think she's good enough."

There was a pause.

"But she is," I said, "isn't she?"

"No better than you!" Sasha turned on me, fiercely. "Don't you go thinking she's better than you are, just 'cos of her uncle and her big loud mouth!"

Sasha is my friend and incredibly loyal.

But all the same, I knew that Starlotta *was* good. I'd never liked her very much, and now she was sort of – well! – my enemy, almost. But it was no use pretending she hadn't "got what it takes".

The more I thought about it, the more depressed I became. How could I hope to get a scholarship when I was up against Starlotta? She is everything that I am not! She is tall and I am short: she is blond and I am mouse. I have freckles and a silly little round face with sticky-out ears like a pixie. Starlotta is all peaches-and-cream with *blue* eyes and a dead straight nose.

My nose is short and blobby, like it was stuck on as some kind of afterthought. Like a lump of Play-Doh. I hate my nose!

I'd once tried sticking it down with Sellotape when I went to bed at night, but all that happened was my face got sore. My nose was just as short and blobby as ever.

Who was going to give a scholarship to someone with a blobby nose?

The others did their best to make me feel better.

Dell said that I must be "strong and positive".

Rosa said that Miss Todd wouldn't have put me in for the scholarship if she didn't think I stood a chance.

Sasha said that Starlotta might be talented

but she had a lousy rotten personality. She said, "You are all bright and bubbly. And you are *funny*. Starlotta loves herself too much."

"Yes, and anyway there are loads of people who look like her," said Rosa. "You're the only one who looks like you!"

"Which is what they want," said Dell. "Somebody *different*."

Unfortunately, instead of making me feel better, it all just made me feel worse! I knew they were only saying these things because they were worried that really I didn't stand a chance.

 The scholarship auditions were arranged for half-term. They were to be held in an old mansion way out in the country. The mansion had been turned into a drama

school, where people went as boarders.

I thought how romantic it must be, and just for a moment I wished that I could be a boarder. But then I thought of Starlight and how happy I was there, and how exciting it was to be right in the middle of London, surrounded by theatres. And a great lump rose up in my throat and wouldn't go away no matter how hard I swallowed.

I couldn't bear to leave Starlight!

Miss Todd had sent all the details to Mum and Dad, including the time of my audition and a map of how to get there. Mum said that she would take a day off from helping Dad pack up the office and would drive me down.

Then I had a real surprise. Well! More of a shock, I suppose you would say. Starlotta came up to me one morning and asked if

Mum would take her to the audition, as well. I was, like, flabbergasted! *Starlotta? Travelling with us?*

"My mum hasn't got a car," she said. "And it's a really long journey by train."

I felt like saying, "So what? It's not my problem if your mum hasn't got a car." But she was being almost humble. I'd never known Starlotta be humble before! I guess it  threw me. I mumbled. "I'll ask my mum."

"You idiot!" screamed Sasha when I told her about it. "You don't want to travel down with her!"

I didn't. It was the very last thing I wanted.

"You're too soft," grumbled Sasha. "You

should have told her to go by train. Then she might have got lost and never turned up. Tee hee! And serve her right!"

"Slow on the uptake," said Rosa and she nodded severely and tapped a finger to her forehead. "You need your head examined!"

That's what I thought, too. I asked Mum, like I'd promised, and I really hoped she'd say that it was too much bother, or the car was going to be full of boxes (from Dad's office). Of course, she didn't.

"That's a good idea," she said. "You'll be company for each other."

"Mum!" I shrieked. "It's Starlotta!"

"You mean, you'd rather she didn't come?" said Mum.

"I can't stand her!"

"So why did you say that you'd ask me?"

"I dunno." I hunched a shoulder. "Felt sorry for her, I s'ppose."

"And now you want me to do your dirty work for you. Is that it?"

I hunched my other shoulder and muttered again that I didn't know.

"Look," said Mum, "there's no law that says we have to take her. But it would seem a bit unkind not to. Don't you think?"

I heaved a sigh. "I guess so."

"She can sit in the back," said Mum. "You won't have to talk to her. You can tell her you want to be quiet and prepare for the audition. She'll probably want to be quiet, too!"

Huh! Mum didn't know Starlotta. Her and her big mouth! She'd be clacking all the way there.

Chapter four

Rosa was right. I needed my head examined! The day of the audition had arrived. Everyone, but everyone, had sent me telegrams. Sasha, Dell, Rosa – both my nans – Auntie Lily – Mum and Dad – even Thomas. It was lovely of them, but it didn't half make me nervous! There were all these people wanting so desperately for me to do well, and here was I, shaking in my shoes before I'd even got there.

I was! I was shaking! Mum had to come and calm me down.

Thomas said, "Give her a slug of Dad's whisky. *I* would!"

But Mum said, "She's going to be all right. She's going to take a *deep* breath and count very slowly up to ten and tell herself that she is going to be a STAR, no matter what!"

Even Mum was at it, now. I had to get that scholarship!

Miss Todd had told us to wear clothes that we felt comfortable in, not clothes that looked good but were too tight or made us hot and bothered or would get all creased up from sitting in the car. She said, "You need to be as comfortable as you can."

Mum asked me what I'd feel most relaxed in, so I said, "T-shirt and jeans". At which Mum raised her eyebrows! But she said I could wear just

whatever I liked. I didn't have
to wear a dress if I didn't want.

I didn't! But Starlotta did.
Wouldn't you know it! She
turned up at our place all
togged out like the dog's dinner. She'd even
got blue sparkly stuff on her eyes!

I immediately felt childish and dowdy
and wished that I could go back and
change, but it was too late. We didn't have
time. I was sure I caught Starlotta looking
at me with a satisfied smirk on her face. I
bet I knew what she was thinking: Sandy
Simmons is just so-o-o babyish!

I thought gloomily that she was
probably right and that I *was* rather
babyish. But at least I could make people
laugh! I do it without even meaning to. I
just say things, perfectly ordinary things,

and they start falling about.

Starlotta *never* makes people laugh. She just makes them gnash their teeth and want to bop her one.

And of course she couldn't sit in the back of the car and be quiet, could she? Oh, no! The big blabbermouth started blabbering the minute Mum pulled away from the kerb. All about what a dear little car we had, it was just so-o-o sweet!

"My uncle has a really big one. He calls it his gas guzzler. You can get ten people in his car."

"My goodness!" said Mum. "What a pity he couldn't have driven you down in it today."

"Oh, he couldn't," said Starlotta.
"He's very busy. He's filming."

"Mum's very busy, too," I said.

"It is so-o-o nice of you to give me a lift,"
gushed Starlotta.

She can really put it on when she wants
to. She opens her eyes very wide and sort of
bats at you with her eyelashes.

Mum didn't seem terribly impressed,
I am glad to say. She seemed more amused,
if anything.

"Please don't mention it," she told
Starlotta. "I'm sure—"

Quite suddenly, without any warning,
Mum broke off and swung the wheel hard
to the right. Fortunately there was nothing
coming towards us. I guess she wouldn't
have done it if there had
been, and then –

then there would have been one little dead
cat.

"*Mum!*" I shrieked. "Stop!"

"Yes, I saw it," said Mum.

"What, what?" cried Starlotta.

"A cat!"

I was out of the door and racing back the
way we had come even before the car had
properly stopped moving.

Lying in the road was the sweetest kitten
you have ever seen! The
colour of apricots, with
a snow-white bib and
little black tips to its
paws. I couldn't see
anything horrid like
blood, but the poor
little thing wasn't moving.

Mum came running to join me.

"It's still breathing," she said. "Quick, Sandy! Run and get a rug from the car."

"What's happening?" demanded Starlotta as I wrenched open the rear passenger door and yanked at the rug she was sitting on.

"Gimme!" I panted.

"Why? What for? What's going on?"

"Just GET OFF!" I roared.

I snatched at the rug and went tearing back to Mum.

"Poor little soul," she said. "It's far too young to be out! Let's roll it very gently on to the rug...gently! That's it."

We all love cats in our family. Well, we love all animals, but cats are our special thing. We would have dozens if we lived in the country!

Mum and I carried the little injured kitten ever so carefully back to the car. We couldn't find any marks on it and Mum said she just hoped it didn't have any dreadful damage inside, where we couldn't see.

"What do we do?" I whispered.

"Well…" Mum paused. She looked from me to Starlotta. "It obviously needs to be taken to the vet just as soon as possible."

"Then let's take it!" I said.

"What, *now?*" Starlotta sounded incensed. "We've got an audition to go to!"

"But it's hurt," I said. "It could die!"

"Yes, and we could be late! And you know what Miss Todd says about being late."

I chewed rather hard at my thumbnail. To be late for an audition is one of the very worst crimes you can commit. But a little cat's life was at stake! Thomas would never forgive me!

I would never forgive me.

"Well, girls, we have to decide," said Mum. "What do we do? Do we go on or turn back?"

GO ON! TURN BACK!

Starlotta and I shouted it together. I bounced round in my seat.

"The vet is only just up the road!"

"But we haven't got *time*!" roared Starlotta. "We'll miss the audition!"

"Sandy?" Mum was still cradling the kitten. "It's your decision."

"Why hers?" screeched Starlotta. "She can miss the audition if she wants. I don't see why I should have to!"

"Starlotta, I'm really sorry," said Mum, "but I can't do what both of you want... I can't turn back and go on. I'm only saying it's Sandy's decision because – well! – you did ask to come with us. If you weren't here, then Sandy would be free to choose."

"I'm a guest in your car!" yelled Starlotta.

"Yes," said Mum, "and a guest usually follows the house rules. Now, Sandy, come on! What do you want us to do?"

I said, "Take it to the vet, Mum. Please!"

We turned the car round and headed back to the vet. He took the kitten in immediately and promised to do his best for it.

"Please don't worry about the expense," said Mum.

"No," I said, "'cos I've got my building-society money!"

Starlotta gave me a look of deepest hate as we got back in the car.

"Well, that's it," she said. "We've missed it now."

Mum drove as fast as she could without breaking any speed limits – Mum is ever such a careful driver. Dad says she drives a car as if it's a baby buggy – but there was just no way we were going to get to that audition on time.

Starlotta sat in the back and sulked. She said the kitten would probably die anyway and we would have ruined our chances for nothing. She said that if you wanted to *get* somewhere and to *be* someone, you couldn't afford to be sentimental.

"You have to be single-minded! You have to want something *so badly* you won't let anything stand in your way."

Mum said, "Wouldn't that make you rather hard and unfeeling? I don't think I should like it if Sandy were like that."

That shut her up! But I knew she was thinking to herself that she had got what it takes and that I hadn't.

Was it really true that I wasn't single-minded enough?

Chapter five

We arrived for the audition almost half an hour late. Starlotta was in the hugest sulk ever. She was in an absolute *mega* sulk. She hadn't even opened her mouth for the last few minutes!

"Don't worry," promised Mum. "I'll tell them what happened."

But Starlotta couldn't wait for Mum! She went charging out of the car and racing ahead of us up the steps. By the time Mum and me caught up with her, she was already babbling out the story to a lady at the reception desk.

"They stopped to take this cat to the vet!
It wasn't my fault! I told them we'd be late!"

"Yes, she did," said Mum. "It wasn't
Starlotta's fault. If anyone's, it was mine."

The reception lady said that she would
"go and talk to Mr Barnaby and find out
whether he'll see you".

She didn't sound terribly hopeful.

Mum and me and Starlotta all sat in a
row in the hall. I chewed my nails while
Starlotta practised smiling and tried to
pretend that she wasn't with us. I whispered
to Mum that it hadn't really been her fault,

it had been mine; but Mum just squeezed my hand and said, "Nonsense! I was the one at the wheel."

It was a comfort to know that Mum was on my side, but I could understand why Starlotta was in such a rage. Not everyone feels about animals the way me and my family do.

After what seemed like for ever, the reception lady came back.

"You're lucky," she said. "Mr Barnaby's agreed to see you."

Whew! What a relief! I looked at Starlotta and grinned, but she only tossed her head and made a sniffing sound.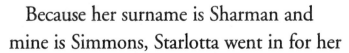

Because her surname is Sharman and mine is Simmons, Starlotta went in for her interview before me. She was there for about ten minutes, and when she came out she was smiling. A *real* smile. Not one of her pretend ones that she does in case someone walks by with a camera. She was happy!

I might as well admit it: my heart *sank*. If Starlotta was happy, it meant her interview had gone well. Mr Barnaby had obviously liked her. He had obviously been impressed by her.

I tried to remind myself that I was me and I could make people laugh.

But I didn't make Mr Barnaby laugh. He wasn't a laughing sort of person. He was very long and thin with a long thin face, all dismal and melancholy, and hands that had the most enormous knuckles. I kept staring at his knuckles all the time he was talking. I couldn't help it! He kept cracking them. They went off like pop guns. Pop! Crack! Click! I half expected them to start firing missiles.

Mr Barnaby wanted to know what experience I'd had, and what I most enjoyed about being at Starlight, and which classes I was best at.

I told him about the Frooties ad and the time I'd danced the Rag Doll in a Christmas show when my best friend Sasha had had appendicitis.

I said that what I enjoyed most about Starlight was being with other people who had the same interests as me, and that the classes I was best at were Mime and Movement (but not Ballet!) and "being

funny and doing impersonations, only we
don't actually have classes in those".

"I see," said Mr Barnaby, and cracked all
his knuckles – pop, pop, pop! – one after
another. "So you're a comedian?"

I said, "I don't mean to be. It just seems
to happen. I say things that I think are
quite ordinary and people start to laugh."

Mr Barnaby didn't laugh. He
didn't laugh *at all.* He just
asked me if I could do one
of my impersonations for
him, so I did Miss Todd
being cross with us
and he didn't even smile.

"Why do you want to go on the stage?"
he said.

By now I was feeling really depressed
because this interview was *not* going well.

But then I remembered something that Miss Todd had once said to us.

"All audiences are different. Some will laugh, some will cry. Some won't do anything at all. Whatever happens, you mustn't let it throw you. Just keep going, and do your best."

So when Mr Barnaby asked me why I wanted to go on the stage, I dragged my gaze away from his knuckles and looked him straight in the eye and said, "'Cos it's the only thing I can imagine doing. It's the only thing I *want* to do. I like it when people laugh, it makes me feel good. And it makes them feel good, too!" I added.

He still didn't smile. He said, "Right, well, I think the time has come for some action."

He led me down a long corridor and up some steps, and suddenly I found myself on stage! I could see there were some people out front. One of them came over to the footlights and said, "Hallo! Sandy, isn't it? I'm Mrs James. I'm just going to ask you and your friend to do a little improvisation for us."

Me and my friend? What friend? I stared round in panic. Surely she didn't mean Starlotta???

She did! Fresh gloom descended upon me as Starlotta came bouncing out on to the stage.

Mrs James said, "Now, you both know what I mean by improvisation, I hope?"

We nodded. We sometimes did Impro (that was what we called it) at Starlight. Miss Todd would tell us to act out a scene "in your own words". I usually enjoyed it – but not with Starlotta!

I don't think she was too pleased, either. I don't think she'd been expecting anything like this.

But worse was to come... I nearly sank through the floor when Mrs James told us what she wanted us to do: she wanted us to act out the scene in the car, when me and Starlotta were arguing about whether to turn back or go on.

I just knew, then, that that was *it*. I wasn't going to get that scholarship.

Starlotta gave me this little superior smile.

We arranged two chairs, one behind the other, and I sat in the front one and Starlotta sat at the back (but making sure the audience could see her. She is not stupid).

This is how some of our dialogue went:

ME: It could die if we don't get it to the vet!

HER: Yes, and I could miss my chance for a scholarship if we don't get to the audition!

ME: But we can't just leave it!

HER: Look, if you want to miss the audition, that's up to you.

ME: I don't want to miss it!

HER: Well, you will, and so will I, and then I'll never forgive you! I want to be an actress more than anything else on earth! I am *single-minded!* I'll do *anything* to get there!

It was like we were having a battle, and
Starlotta was scoring all the points. She was
really full of herself on the way home.

When Dad and Thomas asked me how
the audition had gone, I told them that it
had been DISASTROUS.

Dad said, "Oh, come
on! I'm sure it wasn't."

Thomas said, "Well,
even if it was, at least
you rescued a cat."

Mum had rung up
the vet and the vet had
said the kitten was going to be "just fine".
Mum had promised that if no one claimed
it, we could have it for our own.

I tried really hard to be pleased. I mean, I
was pleased. But all the same, I felt that my
life had come to an end.

Chapter six

The day the letter came, Mum was out. She was helping Dad in the office and me and Thomas were in the house alone.

I was in the kitchen feeding the cats when Thomas came rushing at me, excitedly waving an envelope.

"It's from the scholarship people!"

I snatched it from him.

"How do you know?"

"Says on it…British Drama Foundation. Open it, quick!"

I was so scared, I almost didn't want to. My fingers

were all trembly. I had to force myself.

It was a very large envelope with a whole wodge of stuff inside it. I pulled everything out. On top was a letter, held in place by a red paper clip.

I took one look, and all the blood in my veins just turned to a mush.

We regret to inform you that we do not feel able to offer you a scholarship on this occasion.

"What? What is it?" said Thomas.

I couldn't speak. I just choked and thrust the letter at him, then turned and ran from the room.

I headed for my bedroom, which is where I always go when I want to cry. Seconds later I heard Thomas thudding up the stairs behind me. I knew he only wanted to tell me how sorry he was, but I just couldn't bear it.

Please, Thomas, go away!" I said.

"But, Sandy—" The door came banging open and Thomas galloped through. We never go into each other's bedrooms without being invited. "Sandy, you've got it! Look!"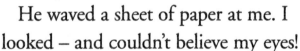

He waved a sheet of paper at me. I looked – and couldn't believe my eyes!

Dear Sandy,

We are pleased to inform you

"But it said 'we regret'!"

"That wasn't you," said Thomas. "That was Starlotta!"

"*What?*"

"They went and put both letters in the same envelope."

"Oh!"

I clapped a hand to my mouth. I'd got the scholarship and Starlotta hadn't – and I'd gone and read her letter!

"Oh," I said, "That's awful!"

"No, it's not," said Thomas. "It's brilliant! You're going to be a STAR!"

"But what about Starlotta?"

"I thought you hated her?" said Thomas.

"Well…I don't exactly *hate* her."

"She was beastly about the cat. She'd have let it die. Just don't worry about her," said Thomas. "Let's ring Mum and Dad!"

So I rang Mum and Dad ("We'll have a celebration tonight," promised Dad) and then I rang Sash, and then Rosa and Dell.

Sasha cried, "Oh, Sandy, what bliss!" Rosa said, "Hooray! I knew you'd beat the socks off her!" Dell said, "Great! So we're still the Gang of Four!"

They were all really pleased for me.

But I kept thinking about Starlotta. I mean, I was sitting on her letter! She didn't know that she hadn't been offered a scholarship.

When Mum came in at lunch time I asked her what she thought I should do.

"Shall I ring her?"

"Oh, I don't think so," said Mum. "I don't think she'd be very happy to know that you'd read her letter. Let me ring the Drama Foundation. Then they can put another one in the post and she needn't ever know."

So that was what we did.

When I went back to Starlight after half-term, my head was way up above the clouds! I was Sandy Simmons and I was going to be a ★S★T★A★R★.

All the same, I was a bit worried about what I was going to say to Starlotta. I know she is a total and utter pain, but I couldn't help feeling sorry for her.

Well! I needn't have bothered. The minute she saw me, she came shrieking across the yard.

"Sandy! I'm so-o-o happy for you! I said to my uncle, now Sandy can have the scholarship. It was just so-o-o generous of him!"

I blinked. What on earth was she talking about?

"My uncle is going to *pay* for me!" gurgled Starlotta. "He just wanted me to try for the scholarship because he thought it would do me good."

Oh, ho ho! What she meant was, he'd been hoping she'd get one so that he wouldn't have to fork out.

I *could* have burst her bubble. I could have told her about the letter. But my head was too high up amongst the clouds! And anyway, it would have seemed a bit mean.

I'd been offered a scholarship! That was all that mattered.

Oh, yes! And I nearly forgot…We kept the kitten! We called him Star, short for Star Struck.

It's what my dad says I am!

About the Author

Jean Ure was still at school when she had her first novel published. She's written lots of books since then, including the *Woodside School* stories and, for older children, *Love is Forever*. As well as writing, Jean really LOVES drama, acting and the theatre! After finishing school, Jean went to The Webber-Douglas Academy and some of her ideas for the *Sandy Simmons* stories come from her experiences there. Jean now lives in Croydon with her husband, seven dogs and four cats.